"MYSTERY OF THE CRYPTS"

Story
by
J. Miller Freeman

Cover art and illustrations
by
Todd Lavender

Akmaeon Publishing, LLC
Cumming, GA

Printed in the United States of America

To Gaye, for whom this book would
not exist without her enthusiastic
inspiration and her
frank honesty.

You are missed.

TABLE OF CONTENTS

PART 1

TERROR OF THE CRYPTS

CHAPTER 1

"...and they *NEVER* found the heads!" Funny Freddy said. Sitting on logs in the forest just out of ear shot from their street, the last rays of sun vanished from the sky for the day. Freddy's two member audience listened intently.

"Wow!" Christopher commented.

"I don't believe him," Christopher's little brother said. It wasn't that Little Ryan was convinced Funny Freddy's tale was fabricated, but such gruesomeness... how could such horror happen here–here so close to home. Hopefully it's not real. Little Ryan looked at his older brother. Christopher was a believer.

Those vanished rays of sunlight had taken with them the last warmth of this late October day. The falling temperature brought its own eeriness into the darkness as the tops of trees vanished into black sky while their roots disappeared in a blanket of rolling, white, creepy fog. Somehow, this setting brought credence to Funny Freddy's story.

Now, Funny Freddy was an under achieving fifth grader. He was passing math but barely, and this was thanks to assigned seating which put Lisa Liu, the math brain, in front of Freddy. Had Funny Freddy not broken his glasses in an unfortunate dodge ball accident, he probably would be making a very suspicious "A" in math. None of Freddy's fellow class mates could attest to Freddy's reading ability. Every school day when Mrs. Werner asked for reading books to be taken out and volunteers to read aloud, Freddy leaves the room escorted to another part of the cavernous school by Mrs. Crowder. Freddy would tell everyone that he would go with Mrs. Crowder in order to read advanced high school novels, but few (if any) believed him. Freddy had difficulty reading *anything*. The broken glasses gave Freddy an excuse which he readily recited to any who questioned his reading skills.

Funny Freddy's one gift was that he held a wealth of local folklore and knowledge. His family had lived in the same small town for generations. Rural streets were often named after Funny Freddy's family members, and every cemetery in town housed at least one if not many of his relatives. No kid would look to Funny Freddy for help with homework and even Christopher had doubts Freddy would be with him next year in sixth grade, but away from school Funny Freddy ruled.

Freddy knew what empty building once held the most awesome video arcade on the east coast; he could tell you why a new high school is being built (the current one is haunted because it is built atop an Indian burial ground). Most recently to Christopher and his brother Ryan, two years their junior, Funny Freddy was telling why the large Victorian mansion that lay deeper in the forest is now vacant. That story had just been told to Christopher and Ryan in the woods.

"Ryan!!! Christopher!!! Come home!!!"

It was the boys' mother. She was out looking for them–a sign that they had failed to heed warnings that they must return home before darkness falls. Oops! The brothers began running toward their mother's voice in hopes that rapidly responding to the call would lessen their impending restrictions.

"Hey, hey..." Freddy called after his colleagues. "Do you want to see the house?"

"Yeah!!" Christopher said while his younger brother simultaneously cried "No!!"

"Ryan!!! Christopher!!! Come home!!!"

"Coming mother!" Ryan's voice echoed through the woods.

"Freddy, we'll talk at school tomorrow," the curious Christopher assured.

CHAPTER 2

The following day over tomato-paste basted rectangular units of flat bread that had been mislabeled on the school menu as "pizza", Freddy further fed on Christopher's imagination.

"They say..." Freddy spoke, each word becoming a more faint whisper. Christopher's head slowly inched toward Freddy's so he could hear in the loud lunch room.

"They say that no one has been in the house since the headless bodies were found."

Christopher's eyes widened.

"Initially, when the meter man came, he looked through the window and saw FOUR headless bodies perched up in chairs around the kitchen table as if nothing had happened–as if they had heads and were about to play cards."

5

Christopher lost interest in his pizza.

"The meter man ran off and called the cops. When the cops got there... Well, we'll just say that one body was missing. The cops only found three headless bodies...but there were four chairs, and I heard that the fourth chair was full of blood and goo."

"Goo?"

"Yeah, goo. It seemed as if the body had just melted into a wad of goo."

Christopher's spoon dropped from his hand splashing into his apple sauce.

"No way!"

"Way! The coroner said he'd never seen anything like it, since... Well he did confess that it happened once before on that very spot in an old shack that sat on the property long before Mr. Crypt and his wife purchased the land and built their mansion. The very same thing happened; that's how the land with the shack was sold so cheaply. The Crypts had just moved into town and didn't know the story."

"Class!" It was Mrs. Werner trying to budge her fifth graders out of their cafeteria seats to return to class for an exciting forty minutes of grammar lessons.

"Is it..." Christopher said trying to get Freddy's attention as the fifth graders shuffled out of their seats into a supposed straight line.

"Is it haunted now?" "Class, quiet!!" charged Mrs. Werner.

6

CHAPTER 3

The boys rushed down the street and found Funny Freddy awaiting them at the gates to the subdivision. He sat on the curb chewing on a long blade of rabbit grass. Rabbit grass was tall foliage that grew just outside the brick and iron gates leading into the subdivision where Christopher and Ryan lived. Freddy called the stuff rabbit grass and said it was good to chew. The brother's mother called the stuff weeds and warned the boys not to chew it as it was sure to cause belly aches.

"Well, what do you want to do?" Freddy asked.

"Tell me more about the Crypt's mansion." Christopher said.

"Do you really want to hear about it?"

Ryan spoke up, "Is it scary?"

"Well it's not scary unless you believe that headless people melting into a puddle of goo is somehow frightening," the old brother responded.

"Come on."

The boys walked down the street and into the forest to their favorite spot, a small clearing in the woods that had logs you could sit on and a growing supply of sticks and planks intended for the future construction of a tree house.

The boys took their respective places on the log seats. Funny Freddy paused patiently for his audience to become comfortable and finish squirming. Once he had their undivided attention, he continued with the tale:

Few people knew this, but a long, long time ago–I believe it was thirty years ago– a new medical examiner was attracted to this area by a strange case. His name was Dr. M. Balmer. Dr. M. Balmer came here to investigate a strange murder. Deep in the woods on the other side of this subdivision, before there ever was a subdivision here, a man, his wife and their two kids were found in the house dead. There bodies were found in their home sitting at a table; their heads were gone. Only three bodies were found. In the fourth chair there was a strange, green glowing goo that smelled so horrible it made Dr. M. Balmer throw up. The case was never solved, but Dr. M Balmer has stayed here as the coroner ever since. He had finally given up on the case. The old house where the bodies had been found began to rot and the roof fell in. Mr. Crypt was a wealthy businessman who moved from the city here to be in the country. He bought the property and bulldozed down the old plank home.

A few years ago, Mr. Crypt, his wife and his two twin sons were found headless in their mansion. Well, once again only three bodies were found– all with their heads missing. In one chair there was a big pile of foul smelling green glowing goo.

"That's not true." Ryan said, trying to convince himself.

"It is true." Funny Freddy confidently remarked.

8

"Prove it."

"Well, the twins were in Mrs. Vanquish's class when they disappeared. Rumor is that the school did not want to use their desks again. If there are two empty desks in her room, then the story is true."

Ryan is in Mrs. Vanquish third grade class. He knows the two desks that are not used. The desks just sit empty in the back corner of the class. Ryan could feel the hairs on the back of his neck beginning to rise.

"So who killed them?" Christopher asked.

"Dr. M. Balmer said it wasn't *who*, but *what* had killed them!!"

Both boys now sat motionless. The sun began to dip from the sky.

"We have to get back or we'll be in trouble." Ryan said, somewhat relieved that his mother was demanding their return before darkness fell.

As the boys traipsed from the woods, Funny Freddy invited "Want to go to the mansion tomorrow?"

The reluctant Ryan remained silent, but his bigger brother, curious Christopher was up to the spooky adventure.

CHAPTER 4

Tomorrow came.

"What are we going to do today?" Freddy asked.

"Let's go..." Christopher enthusiastically started to say.

"No!!" Ryan stopped his brother in mid-sentence knowing that Christopher would plead with Funny Freddy to take them to the Crypt's mansion.

Undeterred by the interruption, Christopher exclaimed "let's go to the old house."

Funny Freddy, sitting on the curb chewing on rabbit grass, took the rabbit grass from his mouth and smiled, he smiled big enough to show his missing upper teeth. "Okay!"

The boys marched through thick overgrown forest. Where trees and bushes left open spots, thick kudzu had crept in slithering along the ground making passage difficult.

"Are you sure you know where you're going?" Christopher finally asked.

"Just look for yellow police tape," the younger brother piped up saying.

The wise Funny Freddy told the boys not to look for yellow police tape. "After all of this time, the wolves have probably eaten the tape."

Ryan moved his eyes from the ground where he was scanning for snakes and quickly raised them to the thick bushes surrounding him, looking for the eyes of a wolf ready to pounce.

As doubt began to fill both brothers' minds about the existence of the Crypt's mansion, an old large house suddenly appeared. Kudzu snaked from the forest through the abandoned yard to the house where it climbed toward the black shingled roof. There were no lights inside the home, in fact the darkness of the windows was so intense it seemed to catch light and hold it imprisoned forever.

The three boys stood starring at the house, amazed. Suddenly, an October afternoon wind stirred, blowing around the house, whistling with an eerie musical composition as it passed through the remains of dangling shutters.

Ryan felt paralyzed.

"Yak! Yak!"

"What's that?" Christopher quizzed.

"Yak! Yak!"

Finally the yak-ster appeared. It was a large black crow that flew just inches over the boys' heads and then came to roost on the eave overhanging the front door. The crow perched himself there and continued to yak almost as if warning the boys to return home.

"I'm going in." Funny Freddy said.

Christopher and Ryan stood ankle deep in thick vines watching Freddy approach the entrance to the Crypt's mansion.

As the distance lessened between Freddy and the door, another stronger wind blew. Startled, the crow yakked as he was nearly blown off of the eave. Suddenly, the front door swung violently open.

Ryan never looked long enough to see if this was opened due to wind, ghost, killer, or monster. Ryan ran like he had never run before. Christopher was torn, but he needed to take care of his little brother. Christopher pursued Ryan as they raced toward home.

"I'm going in!" Freddy yelled at the brothers' backs.

That was the last Ryan or Christopher ever heard of Funny Freddy.

By the time the brothers emerged from the thicket of flora, the sun was setting. The boys ran home to beat the fall of darkness.

CHAPTER 5

Monday morning Christopher awoke eager to see Funny Freddy, but Freddy was absent from the bus. Christopher hoped Funny Freddy was okay; however, when Christopher walked into Mrs. Werner's class, his heart sank.

There was Funny Freddy's desk, moved to the back corner of the classroom, empty and vacant.

"Where is Freddy?" Christopher asked his teacher.

"Freddy is no longer with us." She patted Christopher on the back and asked him to take his seat and open his math book.

To this day, that desk sits in the corner of Mrs. Werner's class, eMPTY!

PART II

RETURN TO CRYPT MANSION

CHAPTER 6

"Arrgghh!" thought Christopher.

"Now come on and give me a kiss," requested Mrs. Reynolds, Christopher's mother.

Christopher's mind reeled: *No sixth grader should have to start the first day of a new school year kissing his mother—especially in the car-rider drop off line. That's for kindergarteners!* Though he kept silent about his feelings, Christopher's body language gave his feelings away.

Ryan, the younger brother, reached up from the rear seat giving his mother a meaningful peck on the left cheek as he grabbed his book bag and quickly exited the car.

"I love you. Have a great day…" the words made it out just before an excited Ryan had completely closed the door.

One brownie point for younger brother! Ryan smiled as he ran toward the school leaving his older sibling wrestling with ideas of how to get out of kissing their mother versus going through with the task without his sixth grade peers noticing.

Then a moment later—"Smaacckk."

"Thanks little brother."

Whatever decision Christopher had made, he had executed it quickly enough to escape the family SUV and catch up to Ryan, slapping him on the back of the head.

Ryan started to respond, but…but looking at his brother Ryan could see that Christopher was trying to hide a pained face.

"Thinking about Freddy?" Ryan reluctantly asked. Walking into the first day of school was probably not the time to talk about their friend who had disappeared mysteriously last year. Of course, Christopher had never seemed to want to talk about his lost friend.

"You know, bro, everybody else was turned to goo. But after Freddy went into that old mansion, no goo was…"

"I know, I know," Christopher said cutting off his little brother. Christopher rubbed the back of Ryan's hair, "Have a good day lil' brother. Maybe we will have the same lunch time."

Going through the door, the brothers parted ways to find their respective classes.

Ryan had been correct. The school was bringing back memories of Freddy; memories that flooded Christopher's every thought as he made his way to his new homeroom, Miss Thomas' room. Turning down the hallway which led to the sixth grade classes, Christopher stopped dead in his tracks.

Is that Lisa Liu? Christopher was shocked over how much the math brain had changed since the end of fifth grade. *That IS Lisa. Wow. She doesn't look like Jackie Chan any more. Gosh. She looks good!*

Lisa turned and waved at Christopher.

Oh I am so busted. Christopher looked down at his watch and started walking fast. *Never thought I would get busted looking at Lisa Liu. Summer was good to Lisa though.* With Freddy pervading his thoughts, Christopher let his mind talk to Freddy's spirit: *Freddy, wish you were here. We'd be fighting to see who sits behind Lisa this year.*

Christopher walked on into the classroom. Ahh…school—schools have an aroma that floats through the air, an aroma of markers, a smell that books emit, and an odor of paint—though if any of the walls had been painted the education department had chosen the same drab colors. This aroma along with the clatter of seeing friends for the first time after three months and the whispers of rumors escaping the already forming clicks brought the realization that summer vacation had come to a sudden halt. By sixth grade, Christopher was a pro at the first day of school.

Christopher looked around; there was no obvious assigned seating. The desks had no names on them. The teacher was not yet in the room. Lisa Liu took a seat, and Christopher quickly took a seat directly behind her.

Freddy, I've got your seat this year.

"Ugh! Look at that!!" The eruption came from behind Christopher all the way from the other side of class. "Does that really happen," exclaimed sixth graders thumbing through a Health Ed book for the first time.

In turning to see who had chosen to sit in the corner of the room, Christopher noticed it. *What?!* There, pushed up against the wall was one empty desk.

"Freddy?"

The name came out in a whisper.

"All right class, welcome to the sixth grade."

The greeting came from the teacher as she entered the classroom.

Oh my gosh! It can't be!

Walking to the front of the class, the teacher took her place in front of the dry-erase board.

"Now class," she said taking the eraser and removing Miss Thomas' name from the board.

"There has been a last minute change, and I will be your teacher this year. Some of you know me from fifth grade, right Christopher?"

The teacher paused and glared at Christopher. He gulped and then slowly nodded.

"My name is Mrs. Werner. I have chosen to teach the sixth grade this year."

Sixth grade? She followed me to sixth grade…and brought Freddy's desk! What's going on?

"All right class, we are going to start out the new academic year with Health Ed. Please take out your health textbooks and open to page six."

Christopher's curious thoughts were put on hold as health education began with photographs of black tarry globs reported to be the lungs removed from dead smokers. Yuck!

CHAPTER 7

Those first few weeks of school went by with no other surprises. Christopher was shocked by the amount of homework he was being given, but his fellow sixth-graders were receiving the same pile of assignments. There was one empty desk in Mrs. Werner's room but everyone, except Christopher, seemed to ignore it, and eventually Christopher's paranoia started to fade.

Math was harder this year—pre-algebra. Christopher had wanted something more to say to Lisa Liu each day other than "Hi", but begging her to help him with schoolwork was not part of his plan. Actually, he lacked a plan to get Lisa's attention, but to admit to a girl that he has trouble with school?

On Friday September 13th, Lisa broke the ice with Christopher.

"My little brother's birthday party is tomorrow. He's in the same class as your brother. I know he is going to invite Ryan. You should come too. That way I have someone to talk to other than a bunch of fourth graders."

Lisa Liu is inviting me to a party at her house? Albeit her kid brother's birthday party, but...

"Uh. Sure, I guess. I didn't know about it so as long as my mom agrees, I'd love to come."

"Class!" Mrs. Werner interrupted. "We have a new addition; there is a new student joining us."

Mary Ann, taking her cue from Mrs. Werner's introduction, walked into the room. Mary Ann was tall and thin—scraggly thin—with long wavy crimson red hair. She wore a blue plaid skirt with matching sweater jacket; this had been a uniform from her last school. Her freckled face appeared more slender than it actually was due to a pair of slightly oversized glasses frames.

"Class, this is Mary Ann Crypt."

Crypt?! Is she related to the Crypts that died in that old mansion? The mansion that...

"Mary Ann is not only now my student. She is my niece."

This girl is Mrs. Werner's niece?

"Oh dear! Mary Ann, we don't have a desk for you. Wait just one minute." Mrs. Werner turned toward the class. "Class, I'll be right back. Please welcome Mary Ann."

A slight glare came from Mrs. Werner, "Welcome her nicely…or be prepared to face the consequences."

No desk?

20

Christopher turned and looked at the back of the classroom where Freddy's empty desk sat up against the wall.

"Okay class," Mrs. Werner walked back into her room followed by a custodian who was carrying a school desk. "You can just sit that desk… uh…just sit it there behind Christopher."

The Crypt girl is going to be sitting directly behind me?

Lisa Liu turned around and leaned her head into the aisle.

"Psst…Mary Ann, I'm Lisa. Want to come to my house this Saturday? It's a party for my little brother's birthday."

The new girl in school who had no friends had already been invited to someone's house.

"Sure!" an enthusiastic Mary Ann replied.

"Mary Ann, Lisa, now is not the time to socialize. Now is the time for learning" directed Mrs. Werner.

Lisa Liu invited the Crypt girl to the party? Suddenly Christopher's invitation seemed less special. *This is turning out to be some other Friday the 13th.*

CHAPTER 8

Mrs. Reynolds was pleased that her boys, especially Christopher, were being socially interactive and making friends. Christopher had become introverted since his friend, Freddy, had...

"Mom!" yelled an impatient Ryan. "Can we go now?"

Mrs. Reynolds had agreed to drive the boys to Shen Liu's birthday party. Christopher had no idea where Lisa and her younger brother, Shen, lived. Christopher was surprised to see his mother turn left as they left the subdivision. Everything else--school, the grocery store, the town--all were to the right. The road to the left led to the woods...woods where the Crypt mansion hid out of sight, abandoned.

Mrs. Reynolds drove past the point where Christopher, Ryan, and the missing Freddy had left the road to traipse toward the old mansion the previous year. That had been the last time Christopher or Ryan had seen Freddy. Though there were reported Freddy sightings from various classmates over the succeeding months, none were confirmed, and Christopher held onto his doubts. After all, shortly after that October night, Freddy's mother and sister were seen leaving town with the family car packed so full of boxes it was presumed she was departing the area with all of her worldly possessions. Freddy's father was not with them, and no one has seen any of Freddy's family since.

Not much further down the road lay the sprawling subdivision where the Liu's lived. Christopher was surprised how close Lisa lived to him, and how much closer she lived to the old Crypt mansion.

Being surprised at Lisa Liu's proximity was one thing; pulling into 2334 Elm Street and being absolutely stunned at the enormity of Lisa's house was another--it had to be the largest home in the subdivision, perhaps even the largest in the county!

"Hello! Welcome!" Lisa called out running to meet her guests.

Lisa was accompanied by the birthday honoree, Shen, and both were followed by their parents. Mr. and Mrs. Liu exchanged cordials with Mrs. Reynolds who promised to return promptly at five o'clock and left her number in case she needed to be contacted sooner.

"Wow Lisa, your house is huge! I thought your parents just work in that dry cleaning shop."

"They *own* that shop--and five others."

"Hey Ryan", called out Shen. "Come on, let's go!"

Boom…boom…bah-boom!

Lisa and Christopher felt the ground rumble. *Boom…boom.* The rumble intensified, and they felt their stomachs vibrate. *Bah-boom… boom-boom-boom!* The noise became audible as an older, but not quite classic, red car with an obvious after-market subwoofer speaker system came screeching into the subdivision. The bass of the music became almost deafening as the red car pulled into the Liu's driveway.

Ryan and Shen had already departed from the driveway running to the back yard to play on large inflatables that had been erected for the birthday party.

Hopping out from the passenger's side of the loud old car was a girl whose hair matched the fading paint on the car.

"Mary Ann, thank you for coming!" exclaimed Lisa as she ran toward the newest guest.

The girls hugged as if they were old friends.

Lisa Liu is much friendlier than I ever thought.

Almost each one of Shen's classmates had come to birthday party. Lisa's friends were limited to Christopher and Mary Ann, but, after all, it was her brother's party and not hers.

Mary Ann waved goodbye to her chauffeur, who incredibly seemed to make the volume of his stereo system even louder as he drove away, now that he was without a passenger.

The afternoon passed quickly. As the sun marched across the sky, the back yard became littered with paper plates dirtied with icing and balloons, some of which had been popped and a couple that had escaped making it all the way into the large oak which towered over the Liu's backyard. Kids had migrated into groups—first divided by age, the largest group was the fourth graders who then were subdivided by school friendships. The smallest group, the sixth graders had separated themselves from the younger kids.

Whatever apprehension Christopher had about being at a party where the only people he knew were his brother, the sister of the birthday boy, and a Crypt girl had slowly eased from this recent convert to introversion. Lisa Liu was talkative and inquisitive. She focused her inquisition on Mary Ann all the while keeping Christopher close to her. Christopher's apprehension was replaced by curiosity.

24

"So Mary Ann, Mrs. Werner is your aunt? Are you close to her?"

"Hmm…not really. My father's job is transferring him to Transylvania, so I came to live with my aunt for a while."

"Transylvania? Transylvania, North Carolina?"

"No. The Transylvania in Romania. My parents are Romanian; guess I will move there with them next year."

"Next year? That's sad. Why not move there now?"

"Well, they want to get settled, and my dad told me my aunt could teach me a lot about our family that I would need to know before moving to Transylvania."

Lisa Liu twisted her lips and cocked her head, "Like what?"

"I don't know," Mary Ann innocently responded.

Christopher piped in, "That seems odd. Your parents think your aunt, whom you hardly know, needs to teach you some family secret before you move with them to Transylvania—Transylvania, home of Count Dracula?"

Mary Ann nodded, "I know. I miss my friends, and I miss my parents."

"*DOO-do, DOO-do, DOO-do, DOO-do…*" Lisa Liu sang the musical intro to the "Twilight Zone."

Mary Ann laughed.

"I'll be your friend, Mary Ann." Lisa Liu said as she reached out and the girls hugged.

Christopher's curiosity was really boiling now. *Mary Ann is a Crypt girl whose family is from Transylvania, home of the most famous vampire in legends, who has been sent to live with her aunt, our weird teacher, to learn some family secret that she NEEDS to know in order to live with her parents in Transylvania. What's up with this girl?*

Honk...Honk...

The trio of sixth graders turned their heads all at once.

"Christopher, looks like your mom is here. I'll go find Ryan for you," and just before Lisa Liu told Christopher, "Thank you for coming," she gave him a kiss on the cheek.

"Hmmh..." grunted Mary Ann as she witnessed the kiss. She didn't conceal the grunt, but it didn't come out loud enough to be heard by her new friends.

Christopher instinctively hugged Lisa Liu bye. Then he turned to Mary Ann and the two engaged in an awkward embrace.

CHAPTER 9

The following Monday at school, Christopher found it hard to concentrate on his school work. He had spent the preceding day and night pondering. *What secrets did Mary Ann's family have? Could Mrs. Werner know something about what's been happening in that old Victorian mansion in the woods? Could she know what really happened to Freddy? Is she involved?* After all, she had followed Christopher to the sixth grade; and he and Freddy had been best friends. *Is Mrs. Werner plotting something terrible against me?* The only conclusion he had been able to make was that he was fairly certain that Mary Ann didn't know anything herself.

Blinngg...

The bell ending the class break brought a terrible surprise--a pop quiz!

"All right class. Put your books away. Take out a pencil. We are having a test today on the science homework you were given over the weekend."

Not only had Christopher failed to do his home reading assignment over the weekend bringing angst to the pop quiz, Mrs. Werner provided additional distraction during the quiz.

Mrs. Werner passed out the tests starting with the students sitting in the front rows who would each then pass the tests back down the rows. Except, Christopher's row was one test short. Mrs. Werner came and handed Christopher's test to him directly. As she did, she whispered, "Hope that birthday party didn't keep you from your reading."

What? Do I detect a bit of sarcasm from Mrs. Werner? Or is this some kind of threat?

Despite his lack of reading on the science subject, Christopher wanted to do well. Christopher was not the math brain like Lisa Liu, but he was pretty good in science. He answered the questions, and despite Mrs. Werner standing beside his desk hovering over him for the entire test, Christopher completed the quiz fairly confident he had done well.

Blinng...Blinngg... The lunch bell rang.

I've got to sit beside Mary Ann and find out what's going on with her family, Christopher reasoned to himself.

CHAPTER 10

Lunchtime did prove interesting. Getting his favorite, rectangular pizza, corn, and applesauce, Christopher picked up his tray. Seeing Mary Ann sitting down, Christopher quickly grabbed the seat beside her.

"Hey, Mary Ann."

Mary Ann looked up giving Christopher a welcoming smile.

"Hey you two!" came Lisa Liu's voice as she took a seat across the table from Christopher and Mary Ann.

"So, I've got to ask you, Mary Ann," curious Christopher coming out of his shell queried, "are you related to the Crypts who were turned to goo in that old mansion?"

"Goo?!"

Mary Ann looked horrified. "What are you talking about?"

"You don't know?" Lisa Liu piped in.

Mary Ann's eyes widened. "Goo?" she asked, even more inquisitively.

"Yeah, goo." Christopher replied. "Well…"

"Years and years ago, the legend goes…" Lisa Liu interrupted Christopher to tell the story. "It's been so long ago many here have forgotten. Mr. Crypt built a big beautiful Victorian mansion in the enchanted forest just outside of town. When the mansion was complete, Mr. Crypt moved his former beauty queen wife, (who still looked gorgeous) and their two twin sons into the mansion. It's been rumored that the twins had strong facial features and the eyes of angels."

Lisa Liu's telling of the story is different than Freddy's.

"Anyway…" Christopher butted in to hurry along the story.

"Anyway," Lisa Liu chimed in over Christopher so she could finish the story, "one day after a big storm, a worker from the electrical company went by the house to check on the power lines, and he FOUND…"

Bling…Bling…Bling…

The lunch bell sounded announcing time to return to class.

"Found what?" quizzed Mary Ann.

"Quiet, class! Now line up," demanded Mrs. Werner.

"Recess—meet at the monkey bars," Christopher turned and whispered to Lisa Liu and Mary Ann.

"Christopher, turn around—**now**!" Christopher turned around and stood straight in line obeying Mrs. Werner.

30

CHAPTER 11

The next two classes dragged by slowly. Time itself seemed to have come to a standstill as Christopher felt Mrs. Werner's eyes staring at him suspiciously. Knowing he had plans to tell his teacher's niece, Mary Ann Crypt, about another Crypt family who met a mysterious and horrific end —a story that seemingly her aunt had *not* told Mary Ann—made Christopher aware of Mrs. Werner's body language.

Finally, *Bling...bling...bling...* The bell rang.

Recess! Recess was always a fun way to end the school day, but on this afternoon, Christopher had business to attend.

While some sixth graders headed to the swings, others organized a furious game of tag. Poor Donnie who had the distinction of being the chubbiest and the slowest kid in the sixth grade had relinquished himself to the idea that he would very quickly end up being *it*, so he went ahead and volunteered to be *it*.

Mr. Ciriatto, the school's principal, would, on warm sunny days, watch the students during recess to give the teachers a chance to stay in their classrooms so that they could grade papers and make lesson plans. This was one of those sunny days; Christopher was glad that Mr. Ciriatto was watching them instead of Mary Ann's creepy aunt.

A bit out of character, Mr. Ciriatto abandoned his normal position of standing in the corner of the playground; rather, he was walking around amongst the students today. Christopher spotted Mary Ann. The two of them glanced at the monkey bars then back at each other and nodded. As they made their way toward the monkey bars, walking slowly to avoid suspicion, Mr. Ciriatto altered his course and went right up to the monkey bars and leaned against them in a standing position. Christopher stopped dead in his tracks. Mary Ann saw the principal standing at the rendezvous point and looked toward Christopher for guidance.

"Pssst…Pssst…" Lisa Liu called out getting her friends' attention.

Lisa Liu had found a new place to meet—the tire swing under the large old oak tree. Arguably, that old tire tied to a rope under the oak tree was the most fun swing on the playground, but because many students had found angry bees protecting unwanted nests in the old tire, few people ventured near the area.

"Come on," she motioned to her comrades.

Meeting under the oak, Mary Ann was eager to hear the rest of the story.

"So what happened?"

Christopher bit his lip to allow Lisa Liu to tell the tale.

"So when the electrical worker got to the mansion, the power WAS out, but not because of the storm."

"Not the storm?"

"No! Not the storm. Someone had **cut** the power lines."

"Whoa!" exclaimed Mary Ann.

Lisa Liu was giving details that Christopher had not previously heard himself. Both Mary Ann's and Christopher's attention were now fully on Lisa Liu. They moved their heads closer together.

"Then," Lisa Liu continued, "the worker looked in through the kitchen window…" She paused briefly for effect. "When he looked through the window, he saw the most horrific scene ever. There were four bodies sitting at the table missing their…"

"STUDENTS!" Mr.Ciriatto had made his way around the playground coming up under the old oak, startling the trio.

"Mary Ann, Lisa…Christopher," Mr. Ciriatto seemed to focus his gaze on Christopher, "I don't want you to get stung."

"Uh…" Christopher grunted looking for words to respond to his principal, but the only words his mind could come up with were 'Stung? Are you involved?' Words Christopher kept to himself.

"Bees." Mr. Ciriatto explained. "There are a lot of bees over here, so watch out."

"Okay." Christopher responded; his paranoia making him start to question even the principal's intention.

Mary Ann and Lisa Liu just nodded politely to Mr. Ciriatto who then walked away continuing his rounds on the playground.

"There were bodies?!" Mary Ann quizzed leaning her head in toward Lisa Liu's.

"Yes!" Christopher took over the story. "And no one ever found the heads."

"The bodies had no heads? Really?!" piqued Mary Ann.

"Really," Christopher went on telling the legend, "and when the police arrived to investigate, not only were the heads missing, one of the bodies had been turned into goo and blood."

"Aarrgh!" Mary Ann grunted in disgust.

"What's more, last year Freddy vanished in that house!"

"Freddy?" Lisa Liu asked a bit surprised.

Christopher shook his head yes. "Yeah, Lisa. Ryan, me, and Freddy went to explore that house. Ryan got scared and ran off. I had to chase after him. The last I ever saw of Freddy, he was walking into that creepy old house."

"They were Crypts?" Mary Ann asked.

"Oh no! I thought that was just a rumor," Lisa Liu said in response to Christopher's story, ignoring Mary Ann's question.

"It was NO rumor!"

"Crypts. My family." Mary Ann uttered as she dropped her head toward the ground.

"Look, it's creepy and weird and I tell you--this school has something to do with it." Christopher averted.

Lisa shook her head raising her arms, "Why? What would even make you think this school has anything to do with such a horrible thing?"

As Christopher started to explain about the empty desks, Mary Ann looked up. "Uh oh, here comes Mr. Ciriatto."

"Kids," the principal spoke up as he neared, "I warned you about being stung. Now please move from here; go join the others."

"Yes sir," came a response in unison from the trio.

Mr. Ciriatto stood under the old oak and watched the three walk away toward the other students.

"Do you think *he* is involved?" whispered Lisa Liu to Christopher as they moved across the playground.

"I don't know, but I have a feeling that Mrs. Werner is involved."

"My aunt?" asked Mary Ann, horrified.

"What desks?" Lisa Liu asked, not giving Christopher a chance to answer Mary Ann.

"You see," Christopher explained as the three walked around the playground, this time keeping moving so as to avoid the principal. "After the Crypt twins met their fate, the school refused to use their desks ever again. Even last year, those two unused desks sat empty in the back of Mrs. Vanquish' classroom."

"Hmm…" said Lisa still listening to Christopher.

"And Lisa, remember--Freddy's desk got moved to the back of the room last year after he disappeared."

Lisa shook her head.

"Well, Mary Ann's aunt, our teacher, Mrs. Scary Werner brought that desk with her into our classroom. It's sitting at the back of the class, and when Mary Ann joined our class, Mrs. Werner had another desk brought in for Mary Ann to use. Freddy's desk is still back there."

"Ahem…" Mr. Ciriatto suddenly appeared, standing in front of the wandering trio. After clearing this throat, "now what are the three of you up to?"

"Uh…Nothing sir," responded Christopher.

"Lisa, Mary Ann, is that true?"

"Oh, yes sir!" Lisa quickly retorted. Mr. Ciriatto looked at Mary Ann who smiled and nodded in agreement with Lisa; though her smile was a bit forced as she felt numbed and a bit frightened by the stories she had just heard.

"This is a playground. Why don't you run and get rid of some of that energy?" The question from Mr. Ciratto seemed more like a command.

The three nodded. Mr. Ciriatto just stood there. Taking the hint, Mary Ann, Lisa Liu, and Christopher ran and joined the game of tag. The three exchanged glances on the playground, but they reserved any further discussion on the matter at hand until the following day.

CHAPTER 12

After dwelling on the stories overnight, Lisa Liu had caught Christopher's paranoia. She had a restless night trying to fall asleep.

At the Werner house, Mary Ann had felt the stern eye of her aunt watching her that evening, but a stern eye from her aunt was a normal nightly occurrence. Paranoia had yet to take over Mary Ann's emotions, but her curiosity was boiling, keeping her also from sleeping through the night.

The stern eyed aunt poked her head into Mary Ann's room.

"You seem anxious, my dear."

Mary Ann nodded her head keeping the suspicions her friends to herself.

"Ah, you just need a good bed time story."

Mrs. Werner strolled into Mary Ann's room and took a seat on the edge of her bed. Mrs. Werner gently stroked Mary Ann's red hair. "Once upon a time, not all that long ago…"

CHAPTER 13

The following morning, Mary Ann entered the class itching to learn more from Christopher and Lisa Liu.

"Let's talk more at lunch; pass it on to Christopher," Mary Ann whispered to Lisa Liu as she walked down the aisle taking her seat.

Christopher sprung into class just before the bell rung.

'Pass it on to Christopher?' Lisa Liu thought to herself. *He sits right in front of her. Why doesn't SHE pass it on?*

"Oh Mary Ann, come on with me."

"Oh no!" Christopher mumbled under his breath as he looked up. "Mrs. Crowder!"

"Yes ma'am." Mary Ann replied grabbing her books and getting up to follow the special education teacher.

Christopher tapped Lisa Liu on the shoulder and whispered into her ear, "Remember last year? Mrs. Crowder used to take Freddy off each day in school—just before he vanished."

Lisa Liu bolted around and grimaced.

"Class!" bellowed Mrs. Werner, stopping all conversation. "It's not time to talk; it's time to learn."

Learn! That's just what we're gonna do; we're gonna learn what's up with you. A grin made its way onto Christopher's face as he made the resolution in his head.

The morning slowly crept by with no return of Mary Ann.

Even Freddy didn't spend this long with Mrs. Crowder; I hope Mary Ann is okay.

CHAPTER 14

Finally, lunch came. Christopher and Lisa Liu took seats at the cafeteria table beside each other.

"Hey...Hey," Lisa Liu nudged Christopher on the shoulder. "Look who's here."

Mary Ann walked over and took a seat at the table across from her two friends.

"Okay. Something weird is going on here, and..." Mary Ann leaned across the table to be able to speak to Christopher and Lisa in a lower voice, "I think Mrs. Crowder is involved. Maybe my aunt, too!"

"What happened this morning?" Lisa Liu questioned.

"I was taken..."

"Ahem!" Mr. Ciriatto's throat clearing was deep, loud, and startled the lunch gang. "You three aren't eating your lunch. Lunch break is short; I want to hear less talking and see more eating.

"Yes sir," Mary Ann said with a shaky voice.

Mr. Ciriatto nodded and continued his policing of the cafeteria— frequently looking back at Mary Ann, Lisa, and Christopher's table.

"We can't talk here!" Mary Ann stated.

"Will your parents, uh and aunt for you Mary Ann, let you guys come to the skate park Saturday?" Lisa asked.

"I think so," said Christopher.

"Um, probably," replied Mary Ann.

"Good, skate park at 10 a.m. Saturday."

Lisa Liu finished talking just as Mr. Ciriatto made another pass by their table.

CHAPTER 15

The following day, Friday, passed without much excitement. Lisa Liu, Mary Ann, and Christopher stayed close to one another, except when Mary Ann was taken for her second morning trip to be with Mrs. Crowder. The trio was cautious to not speak of meetings, mysterious mansions, or empty desks.

With great anticipation Saturday morning arrived. When Mrs. Reynolds arrived at the skate park delivering her sons, Lisa Liu and Shen were already there. Lisa was seeing how high up the half pike she could get her board while Shen was on a flat part working on his Ollie.

Spotting Christopher, Lisa waved.

"Seen Mary Ann?" Christopher asked.

"No, and we've been here since 9:30!"

"Let's wait for her."

"Skate while we're waiting?" The sentence came out of Lisa as a question, but she grabbed her board and hopped onto the half pike not waiting for Christopher's response.

By 10:15 there was still no Mary Ann. Fifteen minutes being an eternity for sixth graders, Christopher was ready to give up when the air around the outdoor skate park started vibrating with *boom…bah-boom*. Lisa Liu and Christopher looked up to see the old red car with faded paint and a loud stereo pulling into the parking lot.

"Mary Ann!" Christopher and Lisa said simultaneously.

With the gang all present and accounted for, the three found a picnic table in the shade and took seats; Christopher's eyes scanned the area for suspicious eavesdroppers. Satisfied that they had found a safe place to talk, Christopher started the conversation by quizzing Mary Ann about what happened when she went with Mrs. Crowder.

"Oh my gosh, Mrs. Crowder's room is just a small office with her desk and three students' desks…and there, on the wall behind her desk, is a framed picture of my great uncle's mansion."

"Your great uncle's mansion?" Lisa Liu asked.

"Yeah," Mary Ann nodded her head—a move that brought her straight red hair over her shoulders covering the sides of her face. Her red hair blended into her crimson sweater looking like a hoodie "…the Crypt Mansion in the woods."

Hmm. Christopher's mind was reeling. *Mary Ann seems to have learned some things about her family.*

"The family you guys told me about was my great uncle and great aunt. I guess those kids were my great cousins."

Lisa Liu's eyes widened, "So what happened to them, Mary Ann?"

44

"Just like you said, they were beheaded. One great cousin's body disappeared…leaving goo as the only clue."

"Did Mrs. Crowder tell you anything about the Crypts or why they are now empty desks in the school —empty desks of kids who vanished in that house?" Christopher asked almost pleading.

"No! But…" Mary Ann leaned her head in real close to her friends'. "Mrs. Crowder goes to a meeting *every* Sunday evening. And so does my aunt!"

"A meeting?" Lisa asked, puzzled.

"Yeah, and I bet if we follow them, we can find out what's *really* going on!"

Christopher listened to Mary Ann's idea of following Mrs. Werner and Mrs. Crowder to one of these secret Sunday meetings; it sounded exciting. Putting his hand to his chin Christopher pondered the possibility of a group of sixth graders following adults in some stealth manner.

Finally he threw up his hands. "How? Just how are we going to be able to do that?"

"Well," Mary Ann spoke up confidently, "You know the boy who brought me here today?"

"The guy in the old car? The same one who brought you to my house for Shen's party?" Lisa Liu asked.

"Yes. He's my cousin."

"Cousin?" Christopher asked.

"Yes, his mom is my aunt—Aunt Scary Werner as you would call her, Christopher."

Christopher and Lisa Liu exchanged glances, and nodded for Mary Ann to continue.

"His name's Ivan. He's eighteen and goes to Middlebrook."

"Middlebrook?" Lisa Liu seemed a bit surprised. "Isn't that the school for…"

Mary Ann filled in the word during Lisa's pause, "…delinquents?"

Lisa Liu just shook her head. Yes, she meant "delinquents", but raising her eyebrows and forcing a smile out of her frown she appeared sorry for thinking it.

"Yeah, it is. Ivan is the black sheep of the Werner family. I don't think he and my aunt get along very well, but he does have a car."

"Black sheep of the Crypt family?" Christopher asked sarcastically.

"Black sheep, white sheep. He's the only person we know with a car who might do this for us. Right?" Lisa interjected.

"Yes." They all nodded.

"Let's do it. Tomorrow??" quizzed Christopher.

The trio made a pact and made plans to follow the teachers to their Sunday rendezvous.

CHAPTER 16

Sunday evening at the Werner house, Ivan and Mary Ann watched as a black sedan inched up the driveway being driven by… the young girl and teenager peered through mostly drawn window curtains… "Mrs. Crowder!" Mary Ann exclaimed spotting her special education teacher behind the wheel of the automobile.

"Where's Mr. Ciriatto?" asked Ivan.

Mary Ann pushed her glasses back up her nose to get better focus. "I think," she said straining her eyes, "yes, yes. Mr. Ciriatto is in the car, but he's riding in the back seat."

Mrs. Werner placed a black formal hat on her head.

"Always looks like she is going to a funeral," Ivan said as his mother exited the house wearing her black hat, black gloves, and matching black dress. Mary Ann just stared at her cousin.

"Let's wait at least fifteen minutes--then we can leave and get the others." Mary Ann bossed her ride. "What time do you have now?"

Ivan looked at his watch. "Hmm…I have 6:66!"

"Very funny," Mary Ann replied sarcastically. "You're sure you know where they go and how to get there?"

"No worries Cuz, I figured that out years ago. It is a Sunday night ritual—they've never missed a Sunday."

Christopher had managed a ride over to Lisa Liu's from his mother, but he had to bring Ryan along with him. Christopher could not figure out a way to tell his mother that he felt his plans for the evening were "too dangerous" for his little brother, so instead he brought him along. Christopher did make Ryan promise to stay outside wherever they went.

Boom-Boom…Bah-da, Bah-da, Bah-da Boom.

Even sitting in the Liu's breakfast nook, they could hear Ivan's car shaking windows in Lisa's neighborhood.

"I think our ride's here!" Lisa exclaimed.

Mr. Liu leered at his daughter.

"It's okay dad. Mary Ann says he's really a good young man."

Christopher looked at Lisa's parents and nodded in agreement with Lisa's statement though Mary Ann had never said any such thing about Ivan. In fact, she had alluded to the possibility that the exact opposite might be true, but anyway, this was their only ride and they needed Lisa's parents' approval to be able to go.

"Wow, that's some loud music!" blurted out Ryan.

Christopher leered at his brother; Ryan got the hint and said nothing further about their ride.

48

"Come on! Come on!" Mary Ann called out, waving as she stepped out of the two door sports car to let Lisa Liu, Christopher, and Ryan into the back seat.

Ivan drove off into the night riding down deserted county roads that the others had never seen before. Ivan suddenly swerved, appearing to head for a thicket of trees.

"Ahhh!!!" Lisa and Ryan both yelled.

Almost hidden from sight of the paved road was an entrance to a dirt road barely wider than a walking path.

"No worries mates," Ivan said as he navigated onto the bumpy hidden road.

"Look!" Ryan cried out pointing to the only hint of civilization—a yellow road sign that read "DEAD END". The sign had been vandalized with the graffiti of a spray-painted sharp-toothed smiley face that looked…evil.

"I think we're almost there!" Ivan called out flipping off his stereo along with the car's headlights. Ivan slowed the vehicle and used the moonlight to see down the narrow dirt road.

"Hey, there's something!" Mary Ann cried out spotting a glowing light up ahead still too far away to make out any details.

"Everyone be quiet!" Ivan commanded.

"Ahhhh!" Christopher gasped. "That's…that's…"

Mary Ann turned around, "The Crypt mansion? Why, yes it is!"

The dirt road had come up to the back of the believed-deserted house which lay deep in the woods. Christopher and Ryan had never seen the back of the house. On their one fateful trip to the place, they had approached from the front through a yard that was now an overgrown field. Here in the back, the dirt road ended in a cleared out spot that was being used for …a parking lot! Ivan slowly and quietly drove up parking his car beside the black sedan that had been driven by Mrs. Crowder.

Several other cars were parked behind the old house which, with light from a multitude of candles shining through windows, looked less abandoned than the Sunday evening Christopher, Ryan, and Freddy had ventured to the place.

"That's Mrs. Vanquish's car!" Lisa blurted out in a loud excited whisper pointing to one of the several cars in the parking lot.

"What do we do now?" Ryan quizzed. Fear eluded Ryan--fear which last year probably had saved him and his older brother from the same fate that befell Freddy.

"'*We*' does not include you, little brother." Ryan said. "You're gonna' stay here in the car."

"Whhaattt?" Ryan babbled.

"Look Lil' Bro, I can't let you go in there. If anything happens to you, Mom will kill me."

Ryan was listening to his brother, but the look of hurt on his face was obvious.

"…besides, we need someone in the car, ready to crank it up and drive like mad back down that path if we come running and hop in. You're the one here who wants to grow up to be a race car driver; you're the best one to man this get away car for us!"

Ryan was a bit contented by his brother's second reason for leaving him outside.

"So?" asked Lisa Liu.

Taking the lead, Christopher said, "So we go inside."

50

Ivan looked at Ryan who had been given the job of watching and waiting in the car, "Guess I'm in with you guys."

Ivan, Mary Ann, Lisa Liu, and Christopher eased their way out of the car and closed the doors behind them being very careful to not make much noise.

"There!" Mary Ann whispered pointing to an open window on the back left of the house. The adventurers tip-toed their way up to the house and peeked through the window. It appeared to have been a bedroom once, but there was no furniture in it now; just possibly a mirror or painting on the wall that was draped with a drop cloth protecting it from the ravages of time.

One by one they climbed through the open window, but as they each stepped into the room, they found the wooden floor creaked loudly each time a foot was sat down on it.

Once in the room, the four stood motionless for a minute. Despite the loud creaky old floor, no one, no monster, and no ghoul came rushing into the room.

Christopher sighed heavily, "Okay, where is everybody."

Mary Ann looked up at Ivan with an inquisitive look. He just shook his head, "I never actually came into the house."

"Wait! I think I hear something." Lisa Liu said cupping her hand to her ear. She inched up close to Christopher.

"Chants! It sounds like chants!" Ivan noted.

Lisa Liu grabbed Christopher's hand and squeezed it. In the dim light of the room, Mary Ann witnessed Lisa taking hold of Christopher's hand. "Hmmph!" She responded not making any effort to conceal her disgruntled gesture from her friends.

"Sounds like those chants may be coming from the basement." Christopher observed. "Come on, let's go see!"

Christopher was the first to poke his head out the bedroom door. After peering down the hallway and slowly moving his eyes around scanning all directions, Christopher stepped out of the bedroom and waved for the others to follow.

The Victorian mansion proved to be a labyrinth of intersecting hallways and rickety doors that led into dusty old rooms. Every door the adventurers opened screeched; each one becoming progressively louder. Yet, no one and no thing came after them.

Turning onto another hallway, *aahh—rhuumm…aahh-rhuumm…*

The chants were now much louder. Mary Ann stretched out her arm and pointed to the closed door at the end of the hallway. The other three looked at her, then looked at each other and nodded. One door now lay between the adventurers and the ritual they had come to investigate.

One more glance at each other, and one by one each person nodded— the nod, a silent agreement to proceed.

As they started walking toward the door, Christopher could feel a lump developing in his throat and his heart began to race.

Lisa Liu's nervousness began to peak too, and she grabbed onto Christopher's right hand to hold it as they made their way to the door. Mary Ann saw Lisa holding Christopher's hand and she quickly followed pursuit and grasped onto Christopher's left hand.

As they arrived at the door, Ivan took hold and twisted the door knob. It twisted…twisted…then finally *click*! The heavy door swung open under its own weight with a loud *sccrreeech*. The noise from those aging hinges sounded like a lion clawing a blackboard.

The adventurers froze in their spots. There were chants coming from behind the door, but no one and no *thing* came rushing out after them. Not even light came rushing from the door—only darkness.

After a few seconds passed, Christopher let go of the girls' hands and walked up to the door and stretched out his neck letting his head slip over the threshold of the doorway.

Mary Ann and Lisa Liu looked at Christopher; from their view he looked headless. They could see the backs of his shoes, back of his pants, back of his torso, but after the shoulders, nothing. Christopher's head vanished into blackness.

Christopher pulled his head back out of the blackness and shook it. "It's too dark. I don't see anything."

Ivan pulled out a flashlight and handed it to Christopher who trepidatiously accepted it.

"Go on!" Ivan said nudging Christopher on the shoulder. "This is what I brought you here for! Right?"

Christopher took a deep breath in, then flicked on the flashlight and started down the steps to the basement. The stairway took him half the way down before it made a sharp turn to the right. As Christopher reached this turn, he paused and then boldly thrust the flashlight in front of him sweeping the light around the entire basement room.

"What!?" Christopher exclaimed.

CHAPTER 17

Outside, Ryan was starting to feel restless…restless and bored, but for now he heeded his brother's command to stay in the car, waiting.

Back inside, Lisa Liu, Mary Ann, and even Ivan responded to Christopher's outcry by entering the darkness of the stairway to the basement.

"What'd you find, Christopher?" Lisa Liu asked as she and the others descended the steps.

"Look!" Christopher said as the others joined him on the landing and he slowly swept his flashlight illuminating the basement from one wall all around to the opposite wall.

"Hmm." Lisa responded astonished, as was Christopher, that the basement was…essentially empty!

Aahh—rhuumm…aahh-rhuumm…

The chants were now loud. Yet, this basement was vacant of people and of furniture except for a bookcase on one wall which held a few old dusty volumes of an outdated encyclopedia and a few old Halloween decorations which lay in weathered boxes.

The group ventured on down the steps into the room. The chants seemed so close they echoed off the walls, but…but there was nothing and no one to be seen that could be the source of the chants.

"I…I just don't understand." Christopher said shaking his head—his fear now replaced with disappointment.

Lisa Liu took the flashlight from Christopher and slowly walked from wall to wall.

"You know…" Lisa said as she explored the room, "this is a small basement." She shined the flashlight all around from the floor all the way to the ceiling. "But it's a big house!"

"Yeah!" Christopher said. He went up to each wall. "Here! Here!" Christopher said standing in front of the bookcase, "the chants are coming from behind this wall. There's a secret room behind this wall!"

"How do we get back there?" Christopher said thinking aloud.

As he said it, Mary Ann came up and started pulling on the books one by one.

"What are you doing?" Christopher asked.

"Seeing if one of these books opens a secret passageway."

"Oh, that's just something you see in the movies…" Lisa Liu said, but as she made the comment, Mary Ann pulled on the "S" volume of the encyclopedia and the wall beside the bookcase swung open revealing a secret passageway.

"Okay. Something you just see in the movies *and* here." Lisa Liu conceded.

Now the adventurers faced a dark orifice; one through which the aroma of candles and the even louder sound of chants could be sensed. The four adventurers scanned each other's facial expressions. It was understood that now, finally, they were close, close to a gathering of souls who most likely know who or what beheaded the Crypt family and caused Christopher's friend to be missing. Of course, this group could be responsible for those actions, and if so, and the adventurers get caught, and…

Christopher reached out and took firm hold of the flashlight; Lisa Liu let go. With flashlight in hand, Christopher turned off the beam and walked up to the edge of the secret passageway. Shoulders touching, the others inched up closely behind Christopher.

"Okay, let's go in," whispered Christopher.

With that, they entered the orifice. Immediately in front of them was a wall painted so black they had difficulty seeing it. The wall meandered about ten feet; the adventures followed it, and THEN …

Christopher, Lisa Liu, Mary Ann, and her cousin Ivan had suddenly emerged from the darkness to find themselves in the midst of the very ritual they were seeking. The chants stopped. Now a multitude of eyes were glaring at them through hooded black frocks.

In the awkward moment of being stared at, each of the adventurers stood motionless except for their eyes which scanned the room.

"Ahhhh!" Lisa gasped putting her hand over her mouth.

Christopher's head sprung around to glance at Lisa, then seeing her fixed gaze he twisted his neck to see what had startled her so. There, on the wall behind the hooded members at this ritual were large glass jars that held…*HEADS*!

56

"Oh my!" uttered Christopher. There were countless jars on the wall.

Those must be the missing heads—there were as many heads as there were empty desks at the school.

Christopher's suspicion was correct, but there were so many heads—many more than he had known to have been killed or to have gone missing.

"Mary Ann!" came a familiar voice from one of the hooded persons who neared the group. "Ivan!" The hooded person pulled her hood down revealing her face.

"Mrs. Scary Werner!" Christopher blurted out.

Lisa Liu leered at Christopher, her facial expressions silently conveying dismay that he just said "Scary Werner" aloud.

"Christopher!" Mrs. Werner called out.

Goose bumps broke out on Christopher's neck, arms, back, and even down onto his legs.

"Mary Ann," came a voice from Mrs. Crowder as she removed her hood and walked up beside Mrs. Werner.

Mrs. Crowder just shook her head, "My dear girl, I was trying to warn you…"

"Christopher," the stern call came from Mr. Ciriatto who also came up to the adventures, removing his hood as he did so. "You are very bright and inquisitive, but …you shouldn't have come here."

The four young people just stood mesmerized by fear and intrigue.

"There are things going on here beyond you—beyond us!" Mrs. Werner interjected.

"See, there is real evil here." Mr. Ciriatto interjected. "LOOK!" he said pointing at the heads in the jars.

"Oh Mary Ann, there is so much for you to know!" Mrs. Werner said.

Ivan looked up. "You too, Ivan."

Christopher found strength and spoke up, "What about me?" grabbing Lisa Liu's hand and holding it up, "and Lisa? Also, what ever happened to Freddy?!"

"Oh my friend…" the voice! *That* voice! Could it be?

A shorter member of the ritual neared, removing his hood.

"Freddy!" gulped Christopher. His heart raced. He couldn't believe it.

"Yes Christopher, it is I!"

A tear started to form in the corner of Christopher's eye. "You're alive! You escaped, Freddy!"

Freddy gazed at the floor. "Alive—yes Escaped no!"

Mr. Ciriatto neared the adventurers. Placing his arm around Christopher, "Freddy is now part of it—he can't leave, not alive. And I fear that since you all have come here, you won't…"

"Wait!" Mrs. Werner interjected, "Ivan and Mary Ann have Crypt blood in them…"

"I don't understand!" Lisa Liu interjected. "What's happening here?"

Mrs. Crowder spoke up to explain, "Years and years ago, long before the Crypt family purchased this land, an Indian, a Native American by the name of Apotamkin, better known as Tamkin, lived on this land. He was infuriated with the movement of settlers into this area. One fateful stormy night he planned an evil attack on the non-Indians who had come to live

58

here. Tamkin sharpened his knives and filled his quiver with arrows. He painted his face with war paint and armored himself with his copper warrior breastplate."

"Copper as you know…" Mr. Ciriatto, the principal and former science teacher, added, "conducts electricity really well."

"Yes." Mrs. Crowder continued, "As Tamkin felt ready to bring his reign of terror upon the villagers he ventured out into the storm, raised his dagger toward the heavens, and then…*Shaarahmm---Boom.*"

Christopher, Lisa Liu, Mary Ann, and even Ivan were mesmerized.

"Lightning!" Mrs. Crowder waved her hands above her head giving visual aid to the tale. "That bolt of lightning came down, attracted by Tamkin's dagger. Then it traveled toward that copper breastplate. Of course, between the two was his head. That lightning bolt took his head off turning it into a charred unrecognizable ball."

"So the lightning stopped Tamkin," Christopher summarized.

"Oh it stopped him, but not his evil spirit." Mr. Ciriatto explained.

Mrs. Werner stepped in to continue the legend, "Now, that spirit seeks revenge, and a new head."

Turning toward one person who seems to have survived Tamkin's wrath, Lisa quizzed Freddy, "How are you alive?"

"I'm part Native American. Tamkin's spirit holds me here, but lets me live as he is trying to recruit me to become part of his continued evil plot."

"And you, Aunt? What are you doing here?" Mary Ann asked turning toward Mrs. 'Scary' Werner.

"Your Great Uncle, Alexandru Crypt, brought with him from Europe knowledge of alchemy and black magic. As he learned of the legend of Tamkin he thought he could acquire this land cheaply and build this beautiful house while protecting his family. He underestimated the evil of Takmin."

"There was another person who survived Tamkin!" Mr. Ciriatto said.

"Well," Mrs. Crowder took her turn to explain. "Alexandru Crypt, his wife, and the twins were not the only ones in the house when Tamkin's evil spirit came…"

"WHO?" asked Mary Ann.

"Your grandfather, my dear. Your grandfather, Alexandru's brother was in this mansion."

"Don't forget about the goo," Mr. Ciriatto reminded Mrs. Crowder.

"The goo?" Christopher asked puzzled.

"Horace Crypt, Mary Ann's grandfather, and her Great Uncle Alexandru Crypt had discovered the goo." Mrs. Crowder explained.

"The goo," the former science teacher elaborated, "the goo is from alchemy--it is magical. It opens doorways to other places.

"…and doorways to the soul" added Mrs. Crowder. "The goo can transport people from one location to another, or…Or it can catch a soul— hold the soul or transport one soul to another body!"

"Transport a soul into another body!?" Christopher repeated Mrs. Crowder's words a bit horrified.

"What happened to my grandfather?" Mary Ann asked.

Mrs. Werner spoke up, "They thought they could trap Tamkin's spirit and escape using the goo; but as you know… They failed. The goo transported your grandfather to his homeland in Transylvania. However, if he comes back to the United States, the goo may actually attract

60

Tamkin's soul to him. Horace Crypt escaped, but not without cost—he can never return."

Lisa's face twisted in her typical puzzled look. "Why does it matter that Ivan and Mary Ann are from the Crypt family?'

"No one other than a crypt has successfully activated the magical properties of the goo—we don't know if it's magical spell will work on anyone else." Mrs. Werner said. "All that is known is as long as the goo is here, and as long as we continue the Sunday ritual, Tamkin's spirit cannot leave this property to wreak the havoc he so desperately wants to bring."

"What about the empty desks at school?" Christopher asked.

Mrs. Crowder, Mrs. Werner, and Mr. Ciriatto looked at each other as if trying to decide who was going to answer the question about the desks, but before they could answer…

"Aaahh!" gasped Lisa. A dark figure approached rapidly.

Christopher looked up and saw Ryan entering the room.

"Ryan!" called out Christopher angrily.

"No! Not Ryan! Behind you!!" Lisa cried out to Christopher.

As he started to turn to look, a flash of shiny light bounced off a dagger now being held high and angled above his head by a large figure wearing a copper breastplate.

"Run Ryan!!" Christopher muttered.

Freddy put one arm around Christopher and instinctively held the other above their heads as the dagger started slicing through the air. Mary Ann leapt toward Christopher and Freddy.

Sswoooffff!!!

"Aaarrrghh!" Lisa Liu yelled covering her eyes.

The dagger swung with such great fury it blew the candles out. The room fell in darkness.

Ryan heeded his brother's words and had already started to run. Silence filled the room. In the silence all that could be heard now was Lisa's scream echoing off the walls and the sounds of a young boy's feet scampering up the stairs.

Mrs. Werner managed to relight a candle bringing illumination back to the room.

"Oh no! Christopher!!" Lisa Liu called out. "Freddy!!"

The dark figure wielding the dagger was gone. There was no Christopher in the room. There was no Freddy in the room. Where the two friends had been standing there was just a puddle of goo.

Mary Ann stood in the corner; Tamkin's dagger was grasped tightly in her right hand.

THE END

Coming soon, from J. Miller Freeman
Second in the
CREAK IN THE NIGHT
series:

Few school days are as memorable in our academic careers as those when

our teachers take us out of the classroom and off on a field trip. Yet for

Arthur, Raul, and Lana, they are about to embark on a field trip into the

paranormal--a field trip they would die to forget. When science meets the

underworld of evil spirits, these eighth graders find the world they know

changing--change which may affect their future; their friends' futures, and

the very souls of all involved. With the fate of the world depending upon

them, can Arthur, Raul, and Lana find the help they need? Can they form

a team and lead this team to defeat the masterminds of evil?

*Read to find out--***If you dare!**